Jane Yolen

Welcome to the SEA OF SAND

illustrated by Laura Regan

G. P. Putnam's Sons · New York

Pronunciation Guide

cholla	*cho*-yah
gambel's quail	gamble's quail
gilas	*hee*-lahs
mesquite	meh-skeet
ocelot	ah-se-lot
ocotillo	oh-ko-*tee*-yoh
saguaro	sah-wá-roh
tarantula	tah-ranch-uh-lah

Thank you to Pattie Fowler of the Arizona-Sonora Desert Museum for
the wonderful help and information that she provided for this book.

Text copyright © 1996 by Jane Yolen · Illustrations copyright © 1996 by Laura Regan · All rights reserved. This book, or parts thereof, may not be reproduced in any form without permission in writing from the publisher. G. P. Putnam's Sons, a division of The Putnam & Grosset Group, 200 Madison Avenue, New York, NY 10016. G. P. Putnam's Sons, Reg. U.S. Pat. & Tm. Off. Published simultaneously in Canada. Printed in Hong Kong by South China Printing Co. (1988) Ltd. Text set in Meridien Medium. The paintings in this book were executed in gouache on illustration board.

Library of Congress Cataloging-in-Publication Data
Yolen, Jane. Welcome to the sea of sand/Jane Yolen; illustrated by Laura Regan. p.   cm.
1. Natural history—Sonora Desert—Juvenile literature. 2. Sonora Desert—Juvenile literature. [1. Sonora Desert. 2. Desert ecology—Sonora Desert. 3. Ecology—Sonora Desert.] I. Regan, Laura, ill. II. Title. QH104.5.S58Y64 1996 508.315'40979—dc20 94-28103 CIP AC

ISBN 0-399-22765-2   1 3 5 7 9 10 8 6 4 2   First Impression

To Beth Meacham and Tappan King,
who introduced me to the Sonora Desert
before and after the rain   —J. Y.

With love for my husband, Peter,
who was with me every step of the way
                              —L. R.

*"Where and how did we gain the idea that
the desert was merely a sea of sand?"*
—John C. Van Dyke, *The Desert*

Welcome to the sea of sand,
a hot sea,
a dry sea,
a rock and stone and sky sea,
where mountains rise like islands
high
above the waves of sand.

But this sandscape
is not just a tan scape!
It's a wash of blue sky,
the splash of terra-cotta sunrise,
the dash of a speckled roadrunner,

a cache of kangaroo rats busy in their burrows,
a scuttle of tarantulas,
a muddle of centipedes,

a huddle of ocelots at noon
in the shadow of a cave,

the late-night wail
of coyote on the trail;

the bleat of spadefoot toads;
the *hissssssss* of gilas;

the whirring *ra-tat-a-tattle* rattle
of a diamondback
warning you off his private track;

and the soft *coo-coo-roo*
of the white-winged dove
standing above
the sea of sand
in its thorny bower
of twenty-four-hour
saguaro flowers.

Welcome to the sand sea,
all-colors-of-the-band sea,
a hot sea,
a dry sea,
green-bush, red-rock, blue-sky sea.
Welcome to the desert
and the rich Sonora land.

The following birds and animals which are not mentioned in the text appear in the illustrations:

jacket	**collared lizards**
pages 6 and 7	**desert tortoise**
pages 12 and 13	**prairie dogs, elf owl**
pages 14 and 15	**humming birds**
pages 24 and 25	**scorpion**
pages 30 and 31	**Harris' hawk**

Did You Know?

The definition of a desert is a place where little rain falls. Deserts cover fourteen percent of the world's land surface.

But just because something is called a desert does not mean that it is deserted. Desert landscapes teem with life: plants, trees, shrubs, birds, insects, and some of the most wonderful animals on the planet roam the sand-and-scrub landscapes. The Sonora Desert, which this book describes, is one of the richest botanical and zoological areas in the world.

But the desert is a place of contradictions. Temperatures may range from below freezing in some places to *well* above 100° Fahrenheit in others. There are rivers in the desert that run swiftly, rivers that run dry in summer, and places where there is virtually no water at all.

To learn more about the Sonora Desert, which covers southwest Arizona, southeast California, most of Baja California, and the state of Sonora in Mexico, get in touch with:

Arizona-Sonora Desert Museum
2021 North Kinney Road
Tucson, Arizona 85743